Think of it like this:

One person watched our video...

And that person liked it enough to tell some friends.

And those people liked it enough to tell their friends...

...Until it caught on like a disease.

Hence, viral!

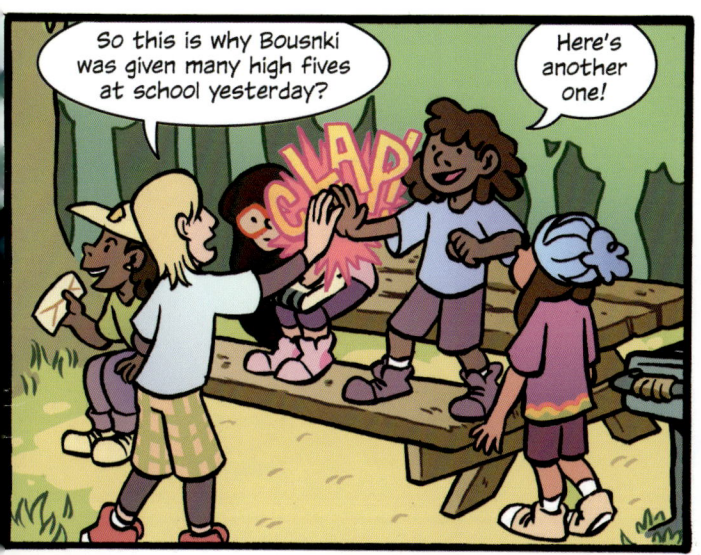

Panel 1: So this is why Bousnki was given many high fives at school yesterday?

CLAP

Here's another one!

Panel 2: After our video went viral, the CEO of a health foods company called Peak Bar happened to see it.

And can you guess what he said?

Panel 3: These kids are stupendiferous! Fabspacular! Wonderific!

If anyone needs a large amount of money to realize their dreams, it's the Loops Crew!

Or my name's not Mr. Peak Bar.

Panel 4: Mr. Peak Bar?

Well, maybe it wasn't exactly like that. But you get the point.

Panel 5: How much money are they giving us, Shorty?

Echem.

Six...

Six?

Panel 6: hundred...

hundred?!?

SIX HUNDRED THOUSAND DOLLARS!!
Guys. Guys? With that kind of money we could all buy new decks! And Nintendo 3DS's! And Apple Watches! And those hoverboard-y things, and, and, and–
We could buy all those things...but we won't. Why?
Because this money is for our new skate park.
Did I hear my name?
your name is skate park?
Loops Crew! Congratulations.
You began your journey stranded on one side of a mighty river.
But with teamwork, creativity, and cooperation, you built a bridge to cross over it.
Thanks, K-Dub! We have enough money for our skate park now!
Urk!

Correction. You almost have enough money for your skate park.
Almost is my least favorite word.
My least favorite word is "can't."
You're more than half of the way there, Loops Crew. Now we just need to push towards the end.
It's time...
It's time to rise up! To make your mark!
For a FUNDRAISER!!!
Well, that was dramatic.
We're going to need some drama, young artiste.
And lucky for you, I'm a master of the stage.

So you really think this will work, K-Dub?

I don't think it will work, Pinky.

I know it will.

BYE FOR NOW!

Enter this portal

for Time Skaters Adventure 7...

FLEUR-DE-WHEEEE!

Morely missed Bounski, yes?

If by missing you mean sleeping, then yes? A lot.

MUSH

Mr. Bounski, it is highly unlikely your reptile wants more than water, nourishment, and relaxation.

Pshhh—silly kitty. Morley is complex personality! Come. We go home, now.

Remember he likes papaya, not kale.

Whoa, whoa, whoa! I thought we were going to talk about the Maker Fair?

It appears Bounski is worn out from your recent adventure.

And I'm worn out from my recent math test...worn out from being AWESOME!

Saving sick dragons, solving sick equations, you've earned a break.

Besides, I think I should like a "cat nap" myself.

Hi guys. Bye guys.

Is that an iguana?

Sketch! So glad you're here!

Do you mean my drawing skills...

Or my *drawing* skills?

Don't worry. I don't need you to conjure any more magic horses or airplanes, or whatever.

The Maker Fair is on the approach! Your drawing skills are going to come in handy.

8

Well that's good. I'm kind of on magic-drawing probation, anyway.
Wuh?
But your power is amazing!
That's the problem, though. A little *too* amazing.
There's such a thing as too amazing?
The other day, Hank told me something:
It's astounding that you can make your drawings come to life now.
But remember, art comes from *inside* you.
And once it leaves, you can't get it back.
Oh come now, that's not how I sound at all.
Like I'd ever be so ***vulgar***.
I said "*creativity* comes from *within* you."
You sure you want to listen to this guy?
How many times must I explain? I am not a "guy," I am a hyper adjusted ninja-hunh?

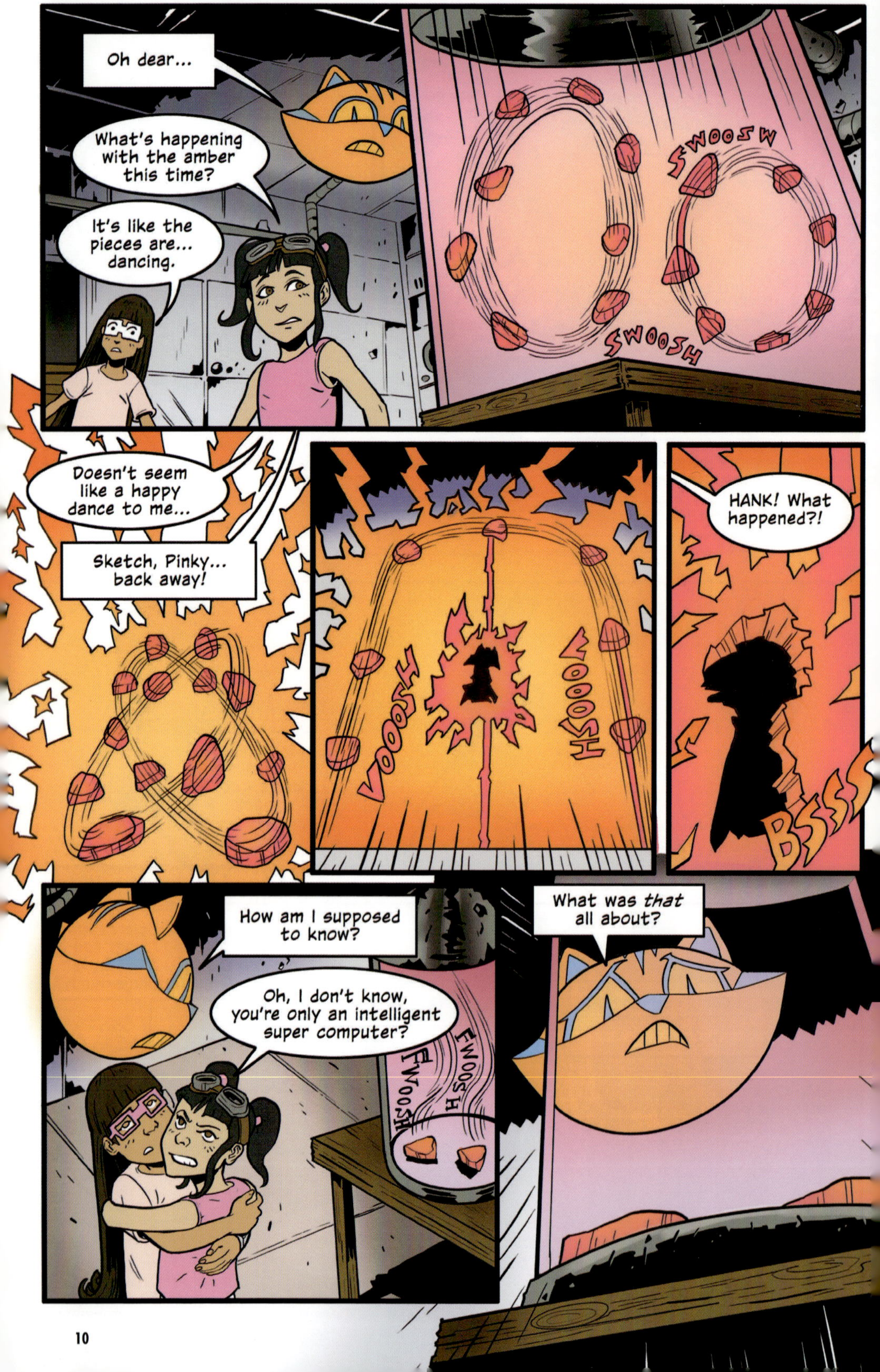

Oh dear...
What's happening with the amber this time?
It's like the pieces are... dancing.
SWOOSH
SWOOSH
Doesn't seem like a happy dance to me...
Sketch, Pinky... back away!
VOOOSH
VOOOSH
HANK! What happened?!
BSSSS
How am I supposed to know?
Oh, I don't know, you're only an intelligent super computer?
FWOOSH
FWOOSH
What was *that* all about?

Argh, no time to investigate now...

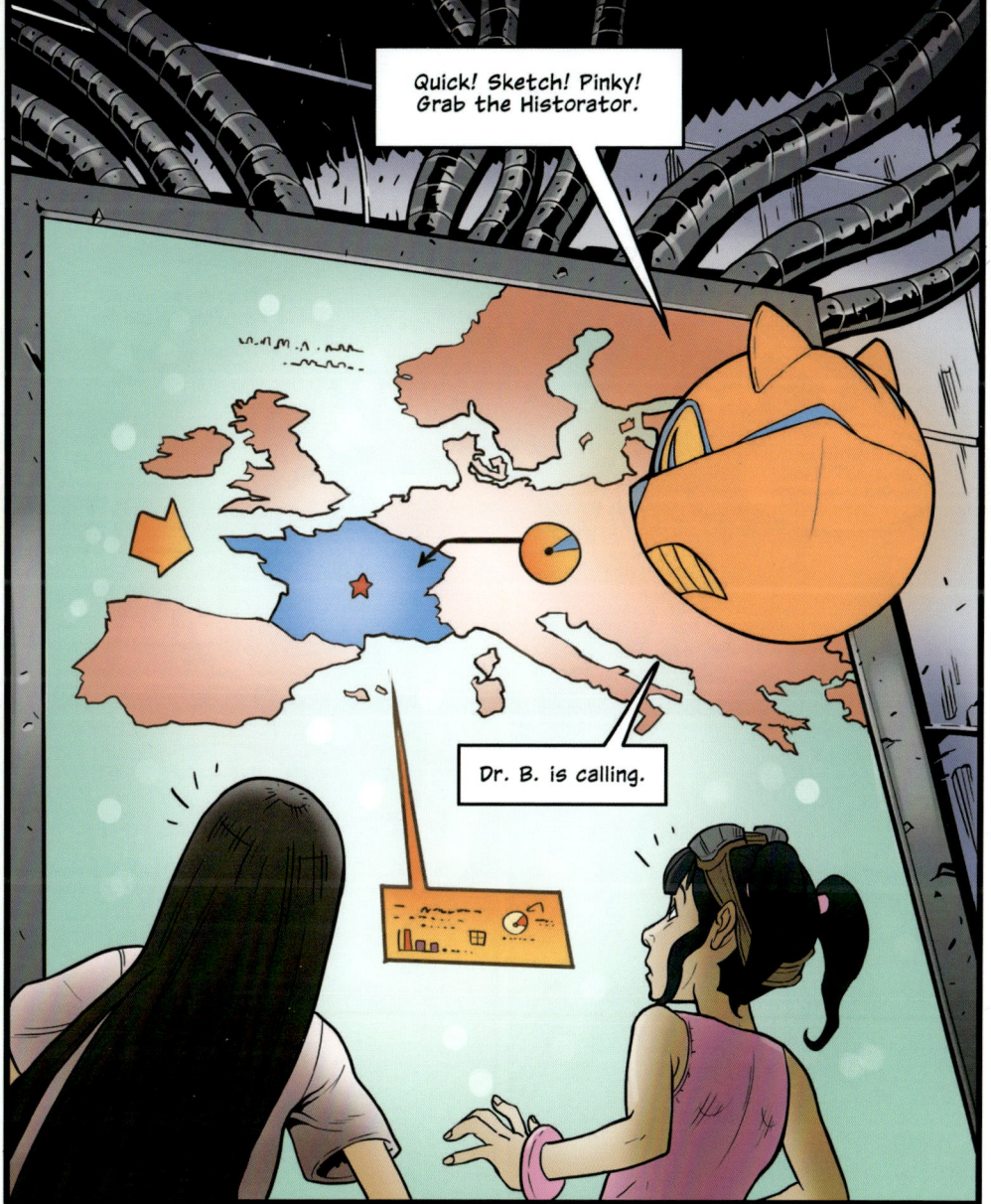

Quick! Sketch! Pinky! Grab the Historator.

Dr. B. is calling.

12

FIRE!!
HANK!
Quelle horreur! Qu'est-ce qu'il se passe?
Parlez-vous anglais?
Please help us!!
D'not move! You will be safe!
A doll?
Shake this doll out the window.
Hurry! Vite, vite! Make sure the audience can see it!
Don't worry. You're not in danger.
It's...how do you say...a ruse?
Mon bébé! Sauver mon bébé!

14

15

FUN-damental Science

MIRACULOUS MUSCLES!
(LES MUSCLES MIRACULEUX!)

From the back of your eyeballs to the ends of your toes, your body is connected, supported, and heated by muscles.

Attached to bone by tough connective tissue called tendons, muscles pull on your skeleton (like strings on a puppet) when you need to move. Without muscles, we wouldn't be able to walk, sit up, or even read a book!

Without muscles, we couldn't breathe, our hearts couldn't beat! We'd just be a heap of bones.

Your muscles are organized as *voluntary* or *involuntary*. All your muscles working together make up the MUSCULAR SYSTEM.

(1) You have have three types of muscle, organized as voluntary or involuntary: Smooth. Named after how they look inside, like your stomach, intestines, and other hollow organs. This type of muscle is involuntary, meaning you don't have to think for them to work.

(2) Cardiac. What your heart is made of. This type is also involuntary. And finally...

(3) ...Skeletal! These are the muscles that move your skeleton, and are voluntary, meaning you DO have to think for them to work.

16

Muscles do four important jobs in your body:

1. Muscles contract (tighten) so your body can MOVE (and your organs can WORK).

2. Muscles attach to your bones to SUPPORT you (and help you BALANCE so you don't fall).

3. Muscles secure your joints in place and give them STABILITY.

4. Muscles work, providing energy to HEAT your body.

YAP YAP

YAY *CLAP*

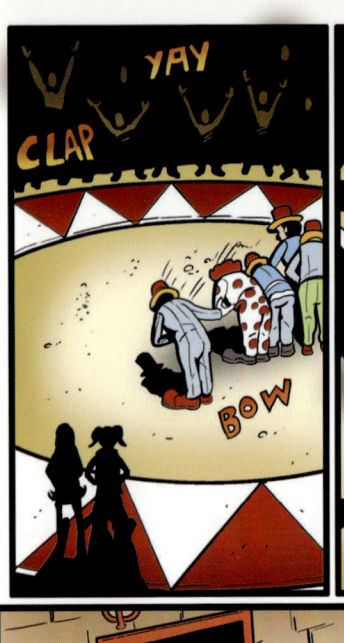

BOW

Monsieurs et madames! La Troupe d'Étienne Calavera!

Well, that was a terrific performance, I must say.

You dropped us onto a burning building, Hank.

You exaggerate. The firehouse gag is one of the oldest in the book, though my online search reveals it began at Ringling Brothers...

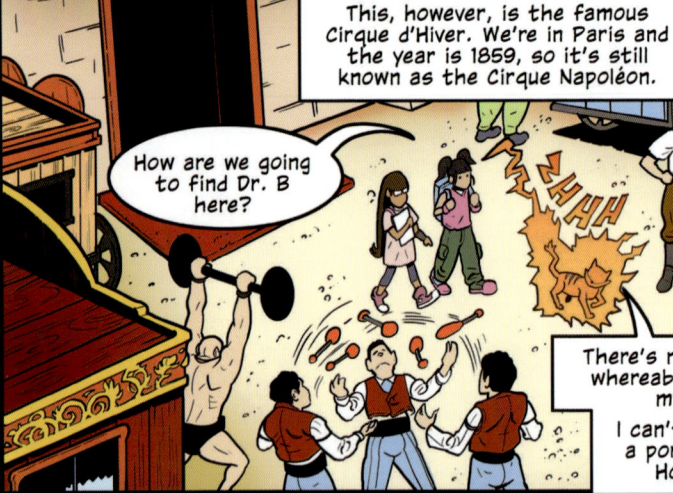

This, however, is the famous Cirque d'Hiver. We're in Paris and the year is 1859, so it's still known as the Cirque Napoléon.

How are we going to find Dr. B here?

SHHH

There's no indication of his whereabouts according to my sensors... I can't even find a portal print. How odd.

Now, there's a majestic fellow. Greetings, esteemed creature!

GRAARRRRR!

There they are! Imposters!

We...we didn't mean to mess anything up!

Hmm?

Eep!

LEAP

18

My dear, what ever are you talking about?
Acrobats?
Surely you must be acrobats of some kind? Mon dieu! How nimble you were.
Well, we do travel off the ground pretty often...
That is excellent news.
For we could use a new flyer or two! Coincidence, no?
Uh...I'm going to say no?
"Flyer" is a term for trapeze artist...
Rrrrhuh?
But, but... Ringmaster...
We aren't really flyers. Not in the way you're thinking.
Pish posh. Your skills have been observed in action.
Léon! Faites attention!
All a true flyer requires is passion. That, and the ability to cooperate!
The trapeze, like dance, combines creativity with sport.
Please see for yourself. The trapeze is up next.
You'll find the body's movement is truly an art!
I like that.
Because it is beautiful!
I've seen the timid become braver than lions! Flying with such abandon, such purpose! Ah, excuse me! I've almost forgotten...
I must tend to my show!

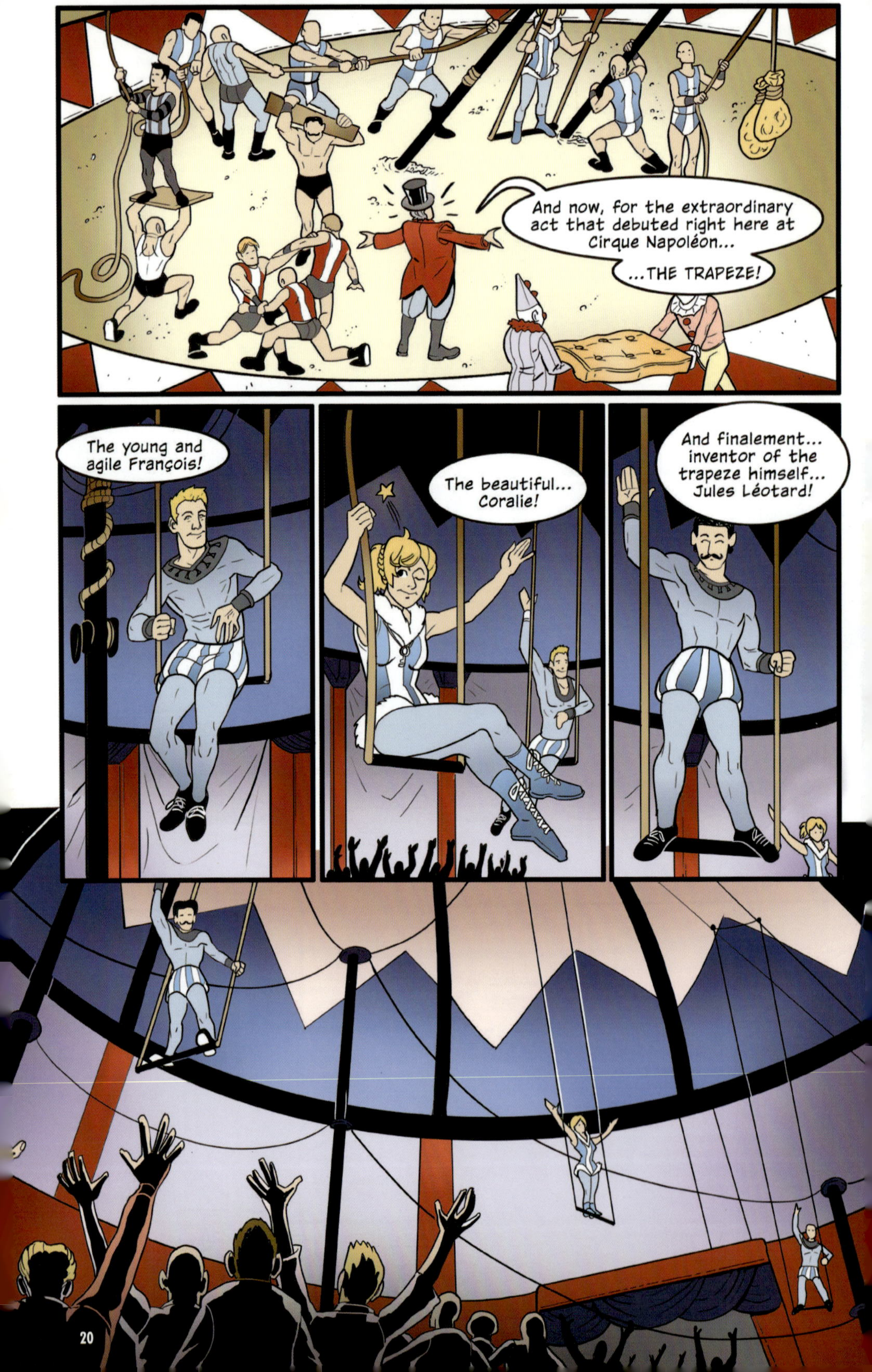
And now, for the extraordinary act that debuted right here at Cirque Napoléon...
...THE TRAPEZE!
The young and agile François!
The beautiful... Coralie!
And finalement... inventor of the trapeze himself... Jules Léotard!

21

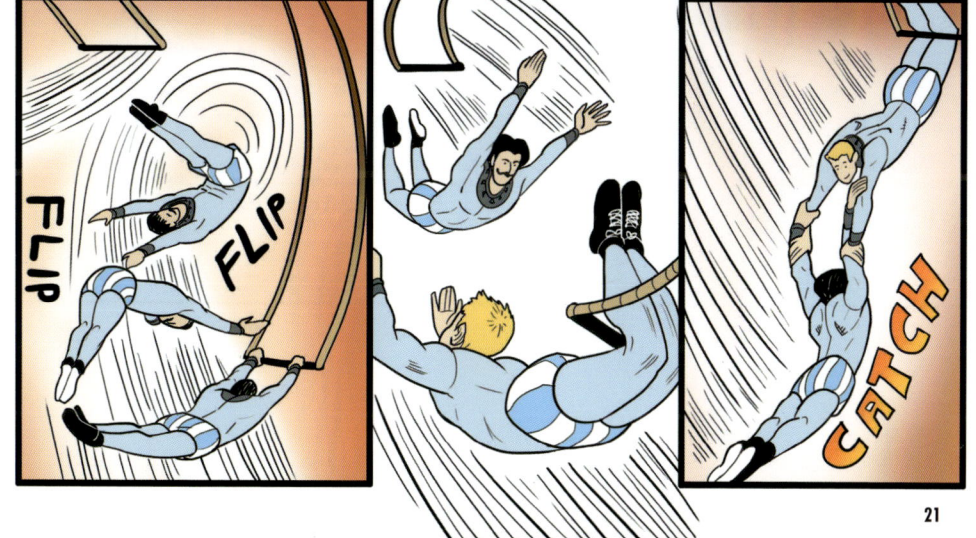

FUN-damental Science

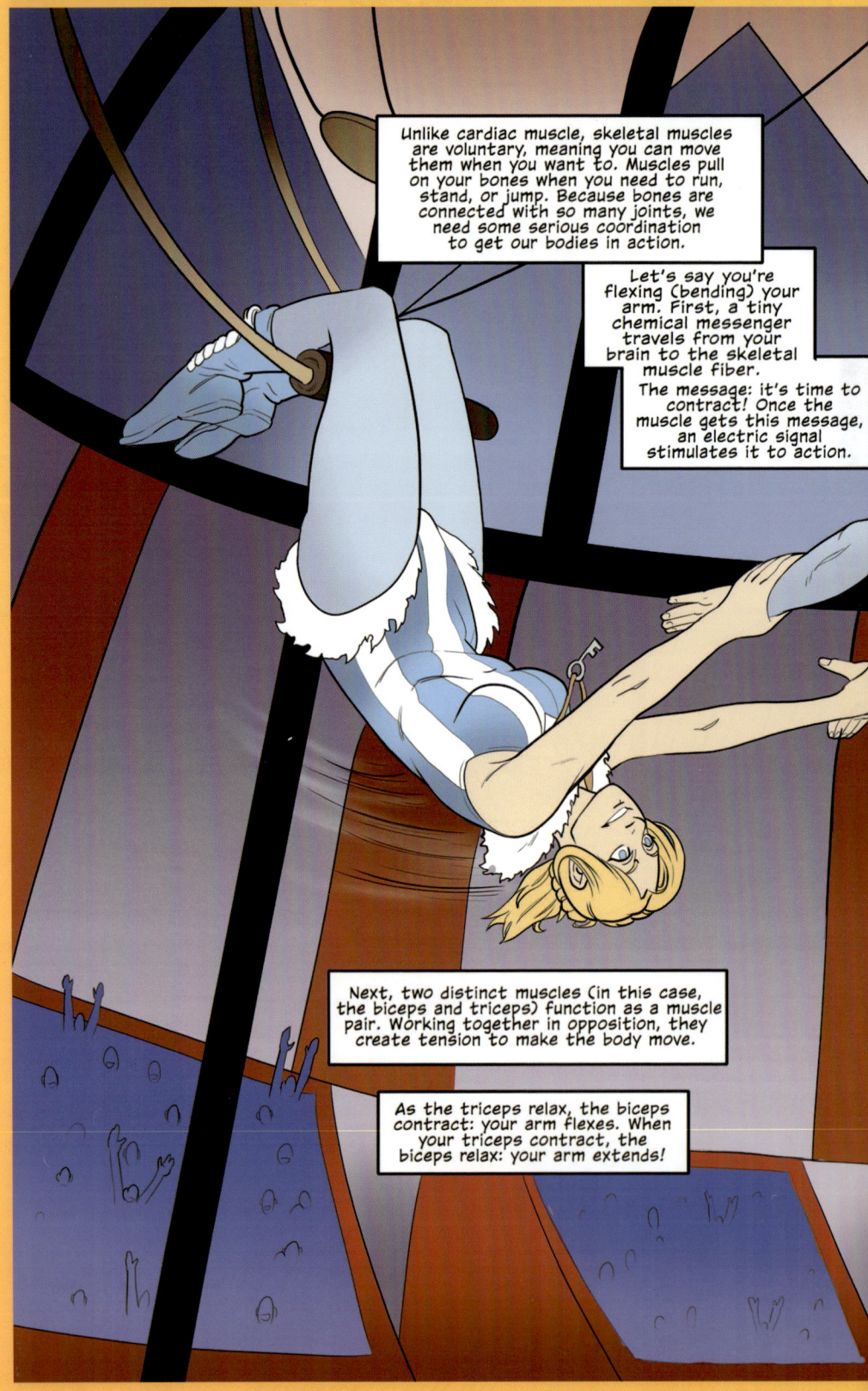

Unlike cardiac muscle, skeletal muscles are voluntary, meaning you can move them when you want to. Muscles pull on your bones when you need to run, stand, or jump. Because bones are connected with so many joints, we need some serious coordination to get our bodies in action.

Let's say you're flexing (bending) your arm. First, a tiny chemical messenger travels from your brain to the skeletal muscle fiber.

The message: it's time to contract! Once the muscle gets this message, an electric signal stimulates it to action.

Next, two distinct muscles (in this case, the biceps and triceps) function as a muscle pair. Working together in opposition, they create tension to make the body move.

As the triceps relax, the biceps contract: your arm flexes. When your triceps contract, the biceps relax: your arm extends!

Opposites Contract...and Relax
(Les muscles opposés se contact et se détends)

Fun Fact/Fait Amusant:

Have you ever heard of muscle memory? If you practice an action over and over, muscles become quicker and more precise in what they do. Your movement becomes more efficient, and actually requires less effort and brainpower. Suddenly kicking that winning goal or hitting a homerun won't seem so difficult!

That was AMAZING!

Yes...

Why don't they have a net?

Because safety nets, it appears, weren't used in the circus until 1871.

Um...mattresses don't seem safe to me when you're that high up.

And now, for the double somersault!

And there is NO way I'm ever doing that!

Wait...

That mattress... It looks like someone's emptied it of filling. That's dangerous!

Pinky the Rope is breaking!

I think you need to use your drawing skills. The super ones. Quick! Before they fall!

But I told you, Pinky, I'm trying not to...

WOOSH

FWISH

24

I understand you don't want to overuse your superpower. We have to be responsible with our abilities.
But think of what Ringmaster LeCouer said about the Trapeze.
You and your art are one, Sketch! Like two acrobats, on the trapeze.
You need to act before they fall or it will be too late!
I typically don't like admitting this, but Pinky has a point.
Alright, you two.
Let's do this.
What am I drawing?
We need a net. That rope is tearing!
Remember what Tianyuan said, Sketch. Remember to...
Breathe.
BZZZ
YES!
SNAP
AAAAHH

26

27

WoAH
Excusez-moi, I believe we can help here!
Léon! Up!
FWOMP
RAWWWRRR!
Roll
Roll
Roll
Très bien!
Encore, Léon!
One more time. Up!
JUMP
Merci.
LIFT
HUG

Are you okay?
You're... you're not hurt?
I am a bit, uhhh, how do you say... shaken up?
Otherwise, I am ready to fly once more, thanks to you!
SLINK
At the circus, there is much hard work and practice...
...movement and joy...
...and sometimes, a bit of luck.
You like it, eh? I only found it a week ago... in the oddest way.
I awoke in the morning, and there it was, around my neck.
I thought it must be lucky.
And apparently, it was.
YAAY
HURRA
Has anyone seen Étienne?

There he is.
But what is he holding?
Étienne?! How could you?
Impossible! I am going to faint.
That key...
SMEAR
Belongs...
To me!!
AHHHH
What did you do with Étienne?
Mandible... I knew it had to be you.
There is no Étienne.
There is only that key. And it is *MINE!*

Stay back, Agent Mandible!
Or what? You'll draw a cage around me?
Or worse!
You children don't understand. That key... It unlocks doors that shouldn't be opened.
Doors to worlds humans should not walk.
Just give it to me, and I vow...
SKSH
You'll never see me again.
I...I don't know.
We can't trust him, Pinky.
Stall for time...keep him talking.
Why do you want the key so badly, Mandible? Why all the secrets?
Heh.
It would be easier for you to give up, you know.
No more running. The key. That's all I want.
BZZ
SWITCH
Fine! Leave us alone and never come back!
FWISH
YES!! AT LAST...
!!
SNIFF SNIFF

?!
Léon! Allons-y!
GRRR
RAWW
KSHH
BZZZ
Good boy, Léon!
His roar is much worse than his bite!
YAAAY

Okay, you two, it's time to get back to the Skelehub. We have new mysteries to solve.
But you're going? And so soon?
I thought you wanted to become flyers? And sail across the sky?
Maybe someday in the future, Monsieur LeCouer.
But I wouldn't worry. Something tells me that people will be flying on the trapeze for years to come.
FIN

FUN-damental Science

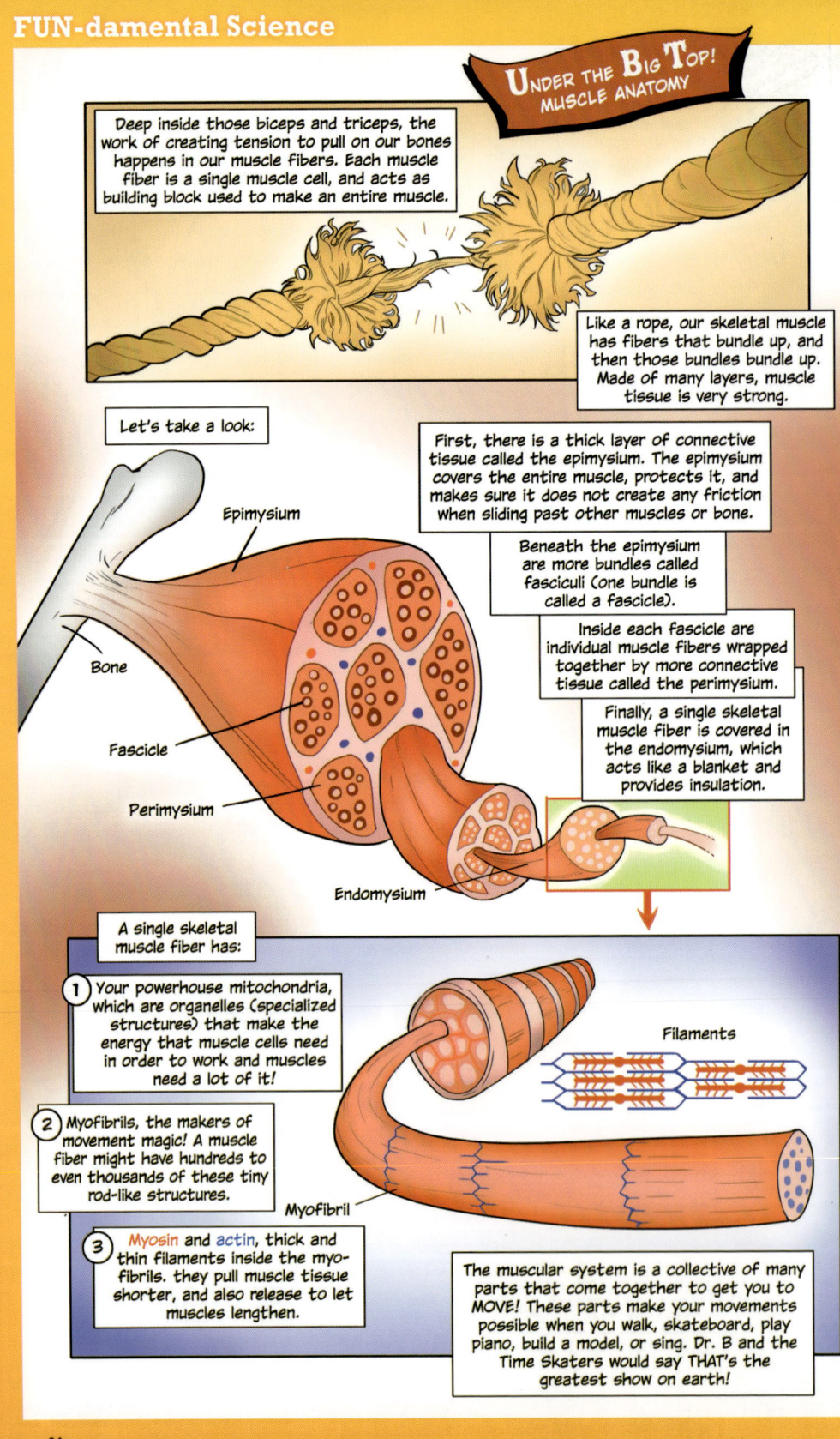

Under the Big Top! Muscle Anatomy

Deep inside those biceps and triceps, the work of creating tension to pull on our bones happens in our muscle fibers. Each muscle fiber is a single muscle cell, and acts as building block used to make an entire muscle.

Like a rope, our skeletal muscle has fibers that bundle up, and then those bundles bundle up. Made of many layers, muscle tissue is very strong.

Let's take a look:

First, there is a thick layer of connective tissue called the epimysium. The epimysium covers the entire muscle, protects it, and makes sure it does not create any friction when sliding past other muscles or bone.

Beneath the epimysium are more bundles called fasciculi (one bundle is called a fascicle).

Inside each fascicle are individual muscle fibers wrapped together by more connective tissue called the perimysium.

Finally, a single skeletal muscle fiber is covered in the endomysium, which acts like a blanket and provides insulation.

Labels: Epimysium, Bone, Fascicle, Perimysium, Endomysium

A single skeletal muscle fiber has:

1. Your powerhouse mitochondria, which are organelles (specialized structures) that make the energy that muscle cells need in order to work and muscles need a lot of it!

2. Myofibrils, the makers of movement magic! A muscle fiber might have hundreds to even thousands of these tiny rod-like structures.

3. **Myosin** and *actin*, thick and thin filaments inside the myofibrils. they pull muscle tissue shorter, and also release to let muscles lengthen.

Labels: Filaments, Myofibril

The muscular system is a collective of many parts that come together to get you to MOVE! These parts make your movements possible when you walk, skateboard, play piano, build a model, or sing. Dr. B and the Time Skaters would say THAT's the greatest show on earth!

CARDIAC MUSCLE: YOUR MAIN SQUEEZE!

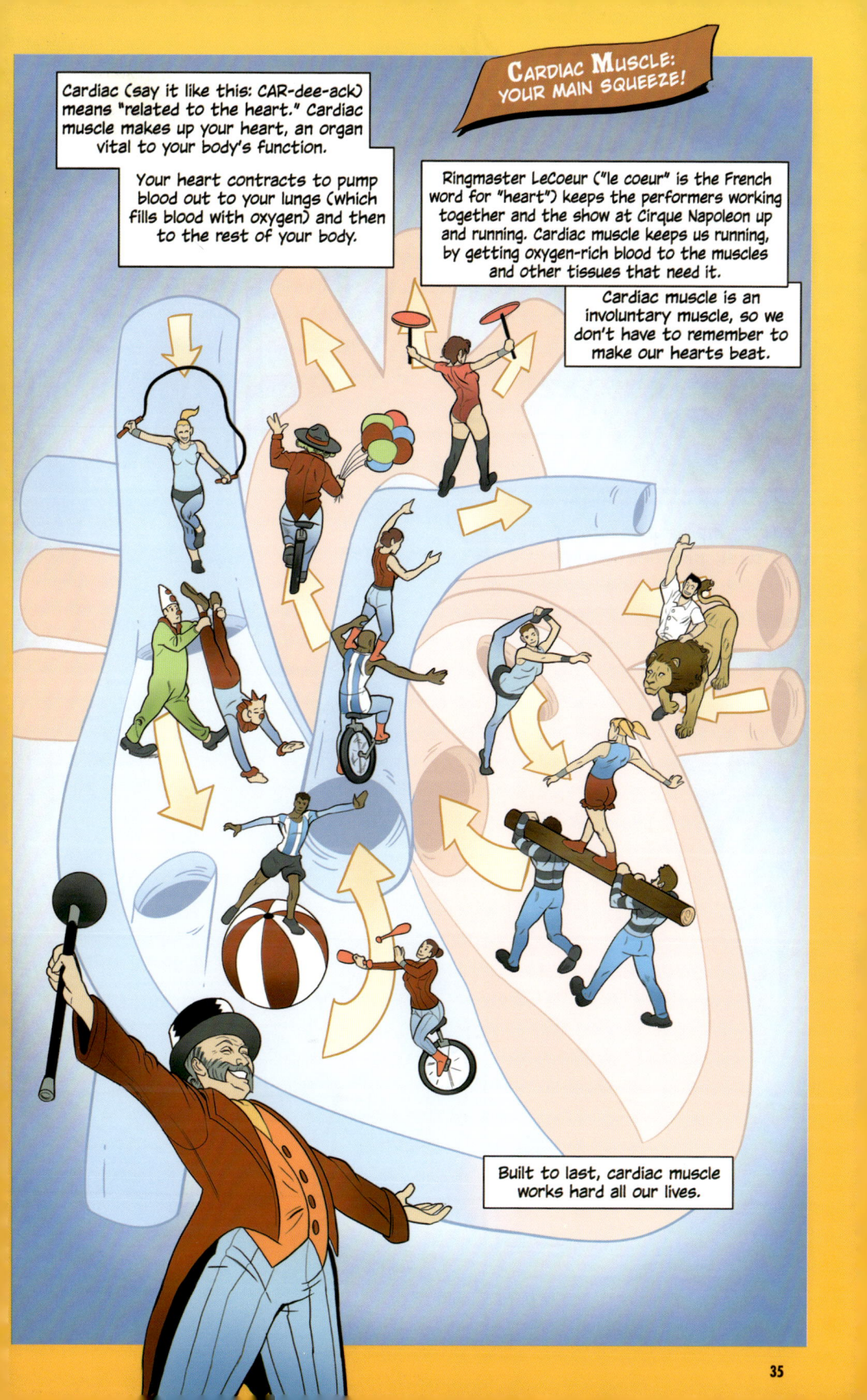

Cardiac (say it like this: CAR-dee-ack) means "related to the heart." Cardiac muscle makes up your heart, an organ vital to your body's function.

Your heart contracts to pump blood out to your lungs (which fills blood with oxygen) and then to the rest of your body.

Ringmaster LeCoeur ("le coeur" is the French word for "heart") keeps the performers working together and the show at Cirque Napoleon up and running. Cardiac muscle keeps us running, by getting oxygen-rich blood to the muscles and other tissues that need it.

Cardiac muscle is an involuntary muscle, so we don't have to remember to make our hearts beat.

Built to last, cardiac muscle works hard all our lives.

35

THE SEVENTH SENSE

ONE! TWO! THREE! FOUR!

Ugh! This is haaard...

Come on, **Sketch**! Exercise is *good* for you!

Muscle robot des...

It's important to be in peak physical shape! No pain no gain!

And if you really think about it, it's **fun**, too!

!

You know what, you're right! This is fun!

500 LBS

That's it, I'm going home.

Great work out!

36